1 MONTH OF
FREE
READING

at

www.ForgottenBooks.com

By purchasing this book you are eligible for one month membership to ForgottenBooks.com, giving you unlimited access to our entire collection of over 1,000,000 titles via our web site and mobile apps.

To claim your free month visit:
www.forgottenbooks.com/free888990

ISBN 978-0-265-78527-0
PIBN 10888990

Latin School Register

VOL. LIX   JUNE   No. 6

SIGILLVM·SOCIETATIS
SCHOLÆ·LATINÆ
BOSTONIENSIS

1940

PUBLISHED MONTHLY EXCEPT JULY, AUGUST AND SEPTEMBER BY THE
STUDENTS OF THE BOSTON PUBLIC LATIN SCHOOL, AVENUE LOUIS
PASTEUR, BOSTON, MASS.

TERMS:—One dollar twenty-five cents per year; by mail one dollar and fifty cents.
Entered as second class matter October 12, 1898 at the Post Office at Boston,
Mass., under the Act of March 3, 1879. Advertising rates on application. Contributions solicited from undergraduates. All contributions must be plainly, neatly,
and correctly written, on one side of the paper only. Contributions will be
accepted wholly with regard to the needs of the paper and the merits of the
manuscript.

CONTENTS

C.H.S.

Literary Board

Editorial . . .
Edward Adelson
Leon N. Hurvitz
Harold Pilvin
Charles Regan
Sumner M. Rothstein
Michael G. Touloumtzis
Paul Mandelstam
Charles W. Tait
Harold T. Coffin

Alumni . . .
Charles Ginsberg
Arthur J. Muriph
Henry V. Strout
Earl M. Wedrow

Photography . . .
Stephen H. Stavro

Cartoonist . . .
Meredith G. Kline

Sports . . .
Bruce C. Ferguson
Daniel Gorenstein

Special Columns . . .
Irving H. Berkovitz
Benjamin L. Gelerman
Bertram A. Huberman
John W. R. Manning
Merton Miller
Lester M. Abelman
Murray Brown
Gerald Posner

Literary Adviser . . .
Mr. Philip Marson

Business

Business Manager . . .
Bert White

Assistant Business Manager . . .
Bert Huberman

Circulation Manager . . .
Melvin Cohen

Associate Circulation Manager . . .
Lester Abelman
Morton Grossman
Arthur Muriph

Circulation Assistants . . .
Norman Fieldman
Harold Greenberg
Myer Horowitz
Arthur Ourieff
Edward Scott
Raymond Seltser
Arthur White
Sumner Yaffe

Advertising Assistants . . .
William A. Silk
Jacob A. Foss
Julian J. Palmer
Harold Polan
Merton H. Miller
Sumner Dorfman
Joseph Coopersmith
John Gerstad

Business Adviser . . .
Mr. Paul J. Wenners

A MIDSPRING NIGHT'S DREAM

The school year has rolled by, and here I find myself in school for the last day of the year. Thanksgiving, Christmas, New Year's, and Easter have gone speedily on their way. For the last few days everyone has been counting the minutes, even the seconds, until school would be over till the Fall. The events which will crowd themselves into your program for the summer—swimming, hiking, camp, and the like—form a continuous movie passing through your mind. Perhaps you are contemplating a trip to one or both of the Fairs, and you can't wait until the happy day when it becomes a reality; or maybe you are imagining yourself at camp, where you will be having the "time of your life."

School is over, and you see the last of the masters and the school until September 12. This, of all days, seems the happiest of the year. On all sides every one is wishing every one else a happy vacation. You rush home in the gayest spirits, only to find you won't be able to go to camp for more than a week. If other days seem to drag, these few days seem to go backward instead of forward. You try everything to amuse yourself; but always the thought "if time would only go faster" is in your mind, although you are aware you can't hurry Old Father Time.

The day before you leave, when you are packing your things, you tingle all over for your first swim. If it was bad packing, it's even worse when you try to sleep that night. You are forever changing your position, and after an hour and a half or more you fall asleep to wake up early the next morning. You can't get on the way too soon. Finally, after what you think many useless delays, you are en route. After going to the station with your parents, you bid them good-by—thinking yourself pretty important to go on a fairly long trip alone. As you watch the countryside fly by, you wonder if anyone else you know will be at camp, and how the water will seem after almost a year since you had your last dip. You reach your destination, and you are picked up by a counselor who was sent to meet you. A few minutes later, when you have arrived at camp, you find other boys. After settling and attending an assembly, you put on your "tights" preparatory for a swim. You rush onto the springboard and dive—you hit the floor with a thud, and you find it was only a dream. For a minute or so you sit stupefied, wishing the dream had come true. Then you think of that test tomorrow, and you are into bed, realizing you have still a few more weeks of school before the good, old summertime.

DONALD LEON, 43.

TENNIS TEAM

Congratulations to the Tennis Team! . . .

It has recently been officially recognized by the School Committee.

Forty-seven candidates, including three veterans, are competing for positions on the Team.

The current schedule includes matches with Rivers, Brookline, Huntington. Roxbury Memorial, Tufts College Freshmen, New Prep., Dorchester, and English; and participation in the Massachusetts Interscholastics.

Mr. Pennypacker is the faculty sponsor.

THE COLORS

An auto parked outside of the School one day last week sported license plates from Texas. The most impressive fact, however, was not that the plates should be from our largest and, from here in Boston, one of our more distant states, but that their colors should be purple and white.

Immediately imaginary bands began to beat and cheer-leaders to cheer; and the Harvard tackle who graduated from the School two years ago was back on the stage with the exciting last quarter when they "only had ninety seconds to play"; and the vision of a group of erudite ranchers strolling over the pampas in ten-gallon hats swapping puns they heard when, maybe, they had Mr. Benson or Mr. Glover, along with the idea of a parade of years when frontiersmen carried our Old Glory into the wilderness and teachers followed who brought the learning of the Latin School into the West.

And it made you swell with pride to know that they speak the same language and listen to the same radio shows and watch the same movies as you do; inspiring to feel that we represent the oldest traditions in education in the United States, that the forms of three hundred five years have been the model for the growth of knowledge on our continent; and that, best of all, our school has shaped the lives and given culture to the free people who live in our America.

There was the vision of a great belt from here to there, and the feeling that any Texan and you had a great deal in common because his number plates gave to the wind the most revered on "the field of many colors"—your colors, Purple and White!

BOSTON PUBLIC SCHOOLS
SCHOOL COMMITTEE
15 Beacon Street, Boston, Massachusetts
CLEMENT A. NORTON, *Member*

March 13, 1940.

Mr. Joseph L. Powers
Public Latin School
Dear Mr. Powers:

I want to thank you for my copy of the REGISTER. It is a fine piece of work and I wish you would congratulate the students of the Public Latin School.

My best wishes to you, your faculty, and the student body.

Cordially yours

C. A. NORTON

A CLASSROOM TRAGEDY

CAST OF CHARACTERS

Homer Slapiens—otherwise known as the "Brain."

Squirt II—favorite quotation is "Never put off for tomorrow what you can do the day after."

Junius Grumbo—goes about with a grudge against humanity in general and anybody in particular.

The Gink—that eminent pedagogue of mathematical science, who will rise to fury at any provocation, but woe be to him who chances to meddle with the first letter of his name.

deBoise—a man of wonderful intellect (everybody wonders about it) known otherwise at de Mob.

Thousands of Others.

Time: 4:30 P.M.

Place: the marble halls of that palace of education; specifically in the now evidently deserted classroom of 2009 (what's an extra zero between friends).

As the curtain rises, we hear voices issue from behind the professorial pulpit, where the Gink stores his test schedules for advance days. (Our friends' interest in the desk is purely artistic, and the only reason they are so intent on the locks is that they want to see what makes the desk open and shut.) Grumbo has inserted a pin in one of the keyholes, and is muttering — "Hmmm — seven to the left—five to the right—one turn back—Hmmm—)

Squirt: A little to the right.

Grumbo: You don't say?

Squirt: Easy now, a little to the left.

Grumbo: Put it to a tune and sing it, why don't you?

Squirt: Here it comes. When you turn it once more, it'll open. Now let me see the test first.

Grumbo: Oh, so now you want to see it first? You'll have plenty of time— after me.

Squirt: Come on! We see it together. 50/50. That's the regular division between capital and labor.

Grumbo: So now you're capital, and I'm labor. That ain't what you said when I found that quarter.

Squirt: Well, it's my pin, and I get first look at the test. *(He makes a violent gesture with his arm, jostling Grumbo and breaking the pin in the lock. The desk shuts with a decisive click).*

Grumbo: There, now you fixed it.

Squirt: You should have let me handle it.

Grumbo: No doubt.

Slap.: When you two stop bickering, try this knife. And if you must squawk, wait till you're outside and aren't waiting for those janitors to creep up behind you. Hurry up. Pry it open. You try it this time, de Boise. These two could kill the afternoon arguing here.

de Boise: O.K. *(Makes a few efficient gestures with knife.)* Ugh! here it comes! *(The drawers spring open suddenly. All spring towards them.)*

Slap.: *(shoving them all aside)* Git out! Think you're getting on a street-car? This is gonna be done systematically. De Boise takes the upper draws. Grumbo, you take the ones on the left, an' to keep Squirt where he won't be tearing your throat out—he stays at the door to watch for our pals the janitors. I'll take the right hand drawers. Now get busy.

Squirt: We'll get a million censures for this.

Grumbo: Shut your mouth. It's bad enough going through all this, and knowing you're getting nothing for all your pains, without having an idiot jibbering in your ear. What do we get here? Security for passing for a few months and then the reckoning in the boards. It all boils down to "them as knows gets," and them as don't wanna work, like us, has to get it this way.

Squirt: We'll get a million censures for this.

Slap.: Lord, will someone throttle him. I know that test must be in the right hand drawers. He keeps all his notes and reminders there. For instance, here's this ship model. (*Pulls a model of a trading ship from a drawer.*) This was evidently a reminder to Gink to attend a prize-fight.

de Boise: Maybe I'm stupid, but how does a ship model remind Gink to go to a fight?

Slap.: Elementary as rolling off a logarithum, de Boise. A prize-fight reminds one of punchers. Punchers are used to clip tickets with; instruments for clipping tickets are called clippers; and clippers are ships; consequently a ship model reminds Gink of a prizefight— Q.E.D. Ya just have to know how Gink works his so-called mind.

Squirt: We'll get a million censures for this.

Slap.: What do you think you are, a chorus? Go to the Glee Club and amuse yourself. But shut up now. (*All this has been rattled off while scholars of the art of locksmithry have been delving into the drawers. Suddenly Slapiens emerges triumphant, a paper in his hands*) Aha! Here it is. (*Reading*) This is what we want. Copy down the pages and numbers of the examples and let's get out of here. (*All work feverishly. The test is copied and restored to its original place and the contents of the drawers are carefully replaced.*

Exeunt All)

Act II

Scene: Rm. 2009 (*We're used to extra zeros by now.*)

Time: The day of the test.

(*The Gink is reviewing the homework with his class of darlings, just before the test. De Boise, Squirt, and Slapiens have a look of self-confidence about them which is unjustifiable in view of their knowledge of mathematics.*)

The Gink: Naow, what was th' answer to th' last one? Did you do it Tan Vesslieri, or did you neglect your home lesson and so force me to give you a Misdemeanor Mark (Ha! ha!) unwilling tho' I am to do so.

Class: Ha! Ha!

Tan Vesslieri: Yes, sir; it was really quite simple. My answer is "492".

Gink: Stoopid!! Get down outa there! Just plain dumb.—Th' answer is "492".

T.V.: (*Here he betrays his naivete and ghastly ignorance, and we lose all sympathy with him.*) But, sir!?? That's the answer I gave you the first time. (*Underlining this sentence is insufficient. It should be printed in red as the glaring faux-pas of the year. And as if this were insufficient, T. V. adds those famous last words—*) But, sir; I know what I'm talking about.

(*This is all. It's the finish. T. V. is never heard of again and it is for the reason of his short career that he was not mentioned in the "Cast of Characters".*)

Gink: (*after a few seconds of speechlessness; but mind, we said only a few seconds. Afterwards come the undepictable explosions.*) Now since we've taken up so much time, you'll have less time for the test (Hah, hah). Here it is: page 248 examples 28 and 29, page 239 numbers 40 through 60, and page 29 numbers 39 and 50. Repeat 'em, Stoopid! (*Class stands up as a man and begins to repeat.*) No, No. I meant Squirt.

(*Squirt repeats pages and numbers.*)
O.K.; go ahead.

(*All start to write zealously except our friends of yesterday at 4:30, that's to say, Grumbo, de Boise, Squirt, and Slapiens. These gentlemen already know the whole test by heart and immediately write out the problems and correct answers without difficulty. All is still, save the scratching of the testees' pencils and heads. De Boise winks to Squirt and whispers "And they say crime don't pay!"*)

Curtain

EPILOGUE

Time: lunch time two days after the test.

Place: Room 2009

Grumbo: (*to Slap.*) Well, this is all right; I got 15 out of 20 in that last test. Only it was a funny thing. Gink left out one example that had been scheduled. Guess he figured we didn't have enough time, and he broke his heart and cut one example out and— (*Just then he is interrupted by Squirt II. This usually calm and steady individual rushes up, his eyes wide and mouth open—truly a wonderful sight.*)

Slap.: yawning. Well, what do you want?

Squirt: What do you know? De Boise just got taken down the office—Gink got him.

Slap.: What! How?

Grumbo: Ha, I knew it. It was bound to happen.

Squirt: Well, it seems he pulled a very clever trick. You know the original test had eight questions, but then Gink cut one of them out leaving seven. But de Boise was so surprised that he knew all the answers and questions that he couldn't help showing off his superior knowledge, and stuck in the extra eighth question for good luck. Now even the Gink could see something was phoney when de Boise gets eight questions right out of seven, so there you are.

Grumbo: You mean there he is.

Slap.: You mean there he was. Ah, well, we can't go into mourning for him. Now what's the story on getting the next German test. I've got it all figured out that——

(*Exeunt*)

Curtain

R. KAY, '41

PARODY ON BROWNING'S IMMORTAL

Oh, to flee from Sweden
Now that Hitler's there,
And whoever wakes in Sweden
Sees, some morning, unaware,
That the nearest fort and the air-raid
    shack
At the termina are full of the pack,
While the red shells scream, and nearby
    burst. . .
This is war—at its worst!
And after the siege, when panic follows,
A part of Germany—what she swallows!
There where my humble cottage stood,
Now smashed to earth and the ground
    scattered over

By bombs and fire—mere splintered
    wood.
That's a wise land; its folk will recover,
Lest you should think they never could
    redeem
Their former self-esteem!
And though the field look wan with shell-
    torn face,
All will be calm when labor makes
    apace,
The peace-time beauty, the only glory—
Far greater than war's fighting vain and
    gory!

W. R. VON BERGEN, '42

"JUST A KID"

Where was he going? He couldn't have told you. Oh, no, not him! He was just walking, walking, walking, endlessly, aimlessly, just walking. But, you say, if he didn't know where he was going, then who did? That is easily answered. No one! But he must have been going somewhere. Yes, he was going somewhere, anywhere, and for the best of reasons. He had just found out that he was "just a kid". He had thought he was quite grown up; a lad of fifteen, a man of affairs. No one had a right to say he didn't know what he was doing. No one! But he'd show 'em! Yes, he would and could! They'd all find out he wasn't "just a kid", as Ethel had claimed! He'd show 'em all, every one of 'em, even Ethel! He'd be famous, a great man, some day! And then, just let 'em say he was "just a kid"!

He had, of course, no definite plan of action. But what he didn't know was that Fate had! At that very instant, Fate was hard at work, preparing his road to success. He couldn't have told you why he was walking on in the dark, aimlessly, yet determinedly. Nor could he have told you why he stopped before that old warehouse, or why he tried the door, or why, on finding it open, he entered. But he did, and for good reason; for Fate was setting the stage for a drama, and he was the principal actor. He didn't know why, when he heard the door open and close behind him, he retraced his footsteps as far as to the first doorway, and went into the room. All he knew was that he was alone, but not alone; bold, but frightened; steady, but nervous. But that's the way of Fate's dramas; the hero glides through, as if in a dream, guided by an unseen hand, yet at all times master of his senses. For a time he heard nothing,

and went out of the room to investigate. But just then, just as he was about to move down the corridor, a man swept past him, panting, groaning, choking. Why he called out, he didn't know; it certainly wasn't the safest thing to do. But he did, and, curiously enough, the man suddenly stopped, swung around to see whence the voice had come, and cried: "No! Don't do it! Please don't Let me out of here! Don't let it get me! save me from it!"

Still acting on impulse, the "kid" stopped still, until he heard the stranger at the door. Then, silently, but recklessly, he made his way down the hallway whence the man had just come. Turning a corner, he saw a light ahead —a weird, dancing, prancing, lurid light, now flaring; now fading; now filling the hall with a dazzling, glaring, blinding radiance, now leaving it in utter darkness. Leaping forward, he hurled himself upon the heavy iron door, threw it shut, and raced back the way he had come. Gaining the door, he found the stranger, struggling with the bolts, locking one as he unlocked the other, and reversing the procedure, time and time again, until even the lad was confused. But he finally solved the maze, and lurched out. The lad seized his hand, crying, "I'm afraid! Help me!"

Why he said this, he knew not, for he wasn't afraid. No, not now. His instinct led him to the alarm box, where he subconsciously pulled the lever. He stayed there, with his companion, as everything began to get less and less vivid. All was now a jumble—the clangor of fire engines, the whining of sirens, the shouting of men, all confused.

But now he was in the police station, the chief beside him, trying to make sense out of what he was mumbling.

"But I'm all right now, I know what I'm about. I know what happened."

"Then suppose you tell us!"

"Of course. It's all very simple. This fellow ran by me in the warehouse, yelling. I shut the door on the one room where the fire was, so that the fire could do no damage to the rest of the fire-proof building. I held *him* for you, and here I am," And then, to himself, "And now Ethel can't call me 'just a kid' any-more, because even the chief says I'm braver than most men, and a lot more sensible!"

HAROLD PILVIN, '40

SONNET

Some say there's no variety in life
That life goes on without the slightest
    change.
To wake is but to see more earthly strife,
That desolation is our vision's range.
"This life of ours is brief, so why delay
To milk it dry and get whate'er we can?"
All this and more—the Sybarites do stay
And so misuse the heritage of man.
Our answer to their stupid blasphemy,
Which finds companionship alone in
  ' those
Who seek to flee their rightful destiny,
Who seek to crush the newly budding
    rose:
"Awake, you fools, to see the bright day
    dawn.
Awake, ye fools, before the morning's
    gone!"

HAROLD PILVIN, '40

SPRING

(*With apologies to Walt Whitman or
    maybe Carl Sandburg*)
Can the junky book
—It's Spring today.
German, bah! See the sun
    in all its glory,
Feel its subtle warmth.
    Spring. Ah!
"Pay attention to your book!"
Tyrant, torturer, bloodless pedagogue!
"Words, words, "I wish to shriek.
"What value when Life is stirring, when
    Beauty reigns?"
But he would only look amazed and
    shocked; Youth left his veins.
And he forgot.
Let me out of here, prison,
Suppressor of my joys!
    Zoom!

HAROLD PILVIN, '40

SLEEP

Have you ever had the experience of falling asleep at an untimely moment? Did you ever lose your self-control to the point where you could not awake at a time of importance? Have you ever had the feeling that some intangible force was putting you into a state of gradual unconsciousness?

One dull spring afternoon my mind was infinitely remote from the uninter-esting topic which was being discussed in the classroom. My eyes were on the open book, but I saw nothing. I was listening to the questions, but I heard nothing. The expression on my face showed enthusiasm, but my mind was a blank. Any response was purely auto-matic.

I was slowly yielding--to the supernatural powers of the Sandman. Someone had seemingly tied tons of iron onto my eye-lids, and try as I might, I could not shake them from my drowsy being.

Again I looked up and saw nothing; again I showed emotion, but felt nothing; again I listened, but heard nothing. I was asleep. I had finally passed into a state of thorough oblivion. I was enjoying the inexpressible pleasures of beautiful slumber.

But my enjoyment was short-lived with the ringing of the bell. Never before had I received such satisfaction in sleeping as I did when I stole some of its pleasures from the classroom. . . .

HAROLD PILVIN, '40

CARELESS

"Hey, there, Joe! Where'd you get that gun?"

The speaker was "Bill" Reade, a tall, ungainly chap of some fifteen years. He evidently voiced the sentiments of "Jack" O'Dell, who, if it weren't for his coal-black hair, which was a striking contrast to Bill's fiery red, would have been taken for his twin. And, for once, "Mike" Sloney showed, by the eager expression on his chubby face and the nervous agitation of his pudgy fingers, that he and his two friends were in perfect agreement. In fact, he even ventured to add: "Yeah! Is it real? Is it loaded? Will it shoot?"

"Take it easy, Infants!" rejoined the one addressed as "Joe". "You'd think you guys were my basses, the way you come around here askin' questions and expectin' me to tell you whatever you want to know! I'll tell you *what* I want to and *when* I want to!"

"Okay, Joe! We know you're bigger than us. We won't meddle in your affairs will we, Gang?"

"All right, forget it! It's my gun. o'course! Paw gave it to me when he died, last year. What with my job and all, I never got a chance to use it, till now. But I lost my job today, and thought I'd clean it up. How do you like it?"

Although addressing his question to the group as a whole, he expected "Bill" to take upon himself the role of spokesman; nor was he disappointed.

"It's a honey, all right. But how do you know it'll work?"

"That, Sonny Boy, is just what I intend to find out!"

So he worked on, the rustic silence interrupted only by the occasional barking of a dog, the squeal of a pig in the nearby pen, or the scurry of a mouse in the walls, roused from his midday slumber by the boys' proximity. All was quiet, until Joe exclaimed: "Yippeeay! Done at last!" And then, as a sort of apology for this outburst, "It seemed as if I'd never be done."

Yes, all was done except to load it, cock it, and fire it; and the test would be completed. He succeeded, without much difficulty, in charging it. Then, as he was cocking it—a loud but muffled roar shattered the midday stillness. Then were heard the excited cries of three thoroughly frightened boys, racing from the shed at full kilt.

The doctor was summoned, but too late. "Joe" Mangan had taken one chance too many. The coroner's report coldly called it an accidental death. But to "Bill", "Jack", and "Mike", it was memorable and tragic.

Lightning and comets were seen when Caesar died, but there was no such heavenly sign for poor "Joe" Mangan. A second before the shot rang out, a rooster had crowed. Thus are the unfortunate, the careless, the lowly, heralded on their way. A rooster crows;‛ the doctor comes; the coroner makes his report; the family and friends mourn; and the world moves relentlessly on.

WILLIAM R. VON BERGEN, '42

EXCHANGES

We acknowledge the following publications:

The "Blue and Gold"—Malden High School, Malden, Mass.

The "Classical Review"—Classical High School, Providence, R. I.

The "Pingry Record"—Pingry School, Elizabeth, N. J.

The "Combermerian" — Combermere School, Barbados

The "North Star"—North High School, Wichita, Kansas

The "Boston University News"—Boston University.

The "Northeastern News"—Northeastern University.

The "Red and Black"—Dorchester High School

The "Botolphian"—Boston College High School.

The "Distaff"—Girls' High School

"Ulula" Manchester Grammar School, ꞏManchester, England.

The "Massachusetts Collegian"—Massachusetts State College

The "Rindge Register"—Rindge High School, Cambridge, Mass.

The "Sphinx"—Centralia High School, Centralia, Ill.

The "Ballast"—Kent Place School, Summit, N. J.

The "Regis"—Regis High School, New York, N. Y.

*   *

Live Today

Yesterday is a memory;
Tomorrow is an imagination;
Today is eternity.
Live today and live forever.
Cut out two days of your life—
Yesterday with its mistakes and follies,
Tomorrow with its fears and dreads,
And live only today.

—The Distaff

*   *   *

Professor Dimbrain has been sent to Egypt to get a story on the Sphinx; Its Life, Habits, and Customs. In his place A. Azzen Anglehook will answer the questions sent in by the readers. He has the angles on everything.—THE EDITOR.

Dear Readers:

I am 'appy indeed, am I, 'appy, to be back, again, writing for you. I 'ave just received a letter from your beloved Professor Dimbrain, w'ich reads—"Dear Azzen. Azzen old friend of mine, I'm glad it's you who will take over for me. Slay 'em, Azzen. I'm safe, etc., and am about to interview Sphinx No. 1,234,567,890¾. Yours, Prof. Iva Q. Dimbrain.

*

Q. Dear Prof.,

What is the ending of that by-line of famous pianists—"They laffed when I sat down to play the piano . . .?

Paddy Rooster

A. Dear Paddy,

". . . but how was I to know that there was no stool there?"

P.D.

*   *

Q. Dear Professor,

Have you had any current experience?

Bud Definitely

A. Dear Bud,

O', my, yes. As you might well suspect, 'aving considered t'e question—t'e good professor was once employed in the Electric Co.

A.A.A.

DOMINI NOSTRI MAGISTRIQUE

MR. McGUFFIN teaches French in 130. . . . Was born May 6, 1898 in Lynn. . . . Went to Lynn Classical, where he was a member of the Debating Team, Dramatics Club and on the staff of the magazine. . . . Attended Boston University, Boston University Graduate School, and Harvard School of Education. . . Was on staff of B.U. Magazine. . . Was awarded the Dallas Lore Sharp Prize for Verse while at B.U. . . Was member of Phi Delta Kappa honorary fraternity at Harvard. . . Has an A.B. from Boston University, A.M. from Boston University, Ed.M. from Harvard. . . Is married and has two children. . . Came to B.L.S. in 1929 from Tunis, where he had been Director of the Foyer de Garçons from from 1926-28. . . Travels extensively. . . Will receive with pleasure a visit from any Latin School Boy or Master who drives through Buzzards Bay. . . Is adviser of the Chess and Checkers Club. . . Has published—"Waltham Book of Citizenship" in 1926, "Lines from Distant Lands" in 1923, and "Primitive English Rhetoric" in 1923. . . .

MR. KLEIN teaches Mathematics in 224 . . . was born in the city of "Red Devils," in 1910. . . While at Chelsea High School engaged in track, but was a most ardent basketball rooter . . . Was captain of the wrestling team at Harvard. . . Received his A.B. in 1932, his Ed.M. from Boston Teachers College in 1934. . . Has been a married man about a year and a half. . . Came to Latin School in 1935 from High School of Commerce. . . Spends his summers as a councillor at Camp Brunonia. . . His hobby is to interchange his golf score with his bowling score. . . Is faculty adviser of the Glee Club and deserves many thanks for his admirable work in the production of "The Mikado."

MR. NEMZOFF teaches history in 223. . . Was born in 1905. . . Is married and has one daughter. . . . Graduated from Latin School and Harvard University, from which he received his A.B. in 1925 and his Ed.M. in 1927. . . Came to B.L.S. in 1929 from Dorchester High School for Boys, where he taught from 1927-1929. . . Is adviser of the Senior History Club. . . In the summer he directs a philanthropic camp for underprivileged boys. Is member of faculty of Hebrew Teachers College. . . Has travelled extensively in Europe, the Near East, this country, and Central America. . . Hopes to visit those regions he has not yet seen; however, he has decided to wait until Hitler stops his game of checkers with the Continent. . . Thinks boys should take advantage of the many extra-curricular activities of the school, for these activities may help them develop interests of permanent avocational or even vocational benefit. . .

YOU'RE NOT SO SMART

1. *Who is the Librarian of the Boston Latin School Association?*

Mr. Dunn   Mr. Henderson
Mr. Levine   Mr. Pidgeon
Mr. Powers   Mr. Benson

2. *Of what school organization is Mr. Kozodoy faculty adviser?*

Glee Club
Mathematics Club
Stamp Club
Highway Safety Club
Literary Club
Detention Club

3. *The Alma Mater Statue in the lower corridor is dedicated to those Latin School boys who died in what war?*

Civil War
Revolutionary War
War of 1812
Mexican War
Spanish-American War
World War

4. *What Latin School Graduate was called "Boston's First Citizen"?*

Samuel Adams
Henry Lee Higginson
Edward Everett
Wendell Phillips
Benjamin Franklin
Ralph Waldo Emerson

5. *Who was the recipient of the Charles E. W. Grinnell Memorial Award in December, 1939?*

Charles Regan   James Springer
Walter Hoar   Stephen Stavro
Malcolm Smith   Ernest Nedvins

6. *Mr. ——— is coach of the Tennis Team.*

Mr. C. Fitzgerald   Mr. Klein
Mr. Gordon   Mr. Cannell
Mr. Dolan   Mr. Pennypacker

7. *How many points are necessary for promotion from the freshman year?*

500   900   850   1000   150
950   750   800   75   89

8. *What member of the graduating class of 1939 accepted the Arthur Irving Fiske Scholarship but refused the stipend?*

Joel Cohen   Joseph Zilber
Arthur Vershbow   Russell Robinson
Jacob Levenson   Sidney Siegal

9. *Who is the most recent master appointed to the History Department in this school?*

Mr. French   Mr. Godfrey
Mr. Peirce   Mr. Murphy
Mr. Rosenthal   Mr. Nemzoff

10. *What Head Master is responsible for the misdemeanor mark as an "institution"?*

Head Master Cheever
Head Master Lovell
Head Master Gould
Head Master Powers
Head Master Pennypacker
Head Master Jones

LATIN SCHOOL BOYS

C.E.E.B. Results

It is the custom each year to present to the boys of Latin School, the names of their fellow-students who have received the highest marks in the College Entrance Board examinations. Following is a list of boys, who received *Highest Honors* (ie., above 90%) in the examinations specified in 1939. The boys are listed in the order of their rank.

ENGLISH—Jacob C. Levenson, Elihu Z. Rubin, Gerard F. Colleran, Franklin N. Flaschner.

LATIN H—Jacob C. Levenson.

LATIN 3—Leonard Wolsky, Sumner M. Rothstein, Charles Ginsberg, Arthur

Q. Neyhus, Leon N. Hurvitz, Robert Kagan, Daniel G. Mostow, Thomas F. Casey, Richard E. Potocki Lenin A. Baler, Herman E. Grossman, Seymour Fried, Daniel Gorenstein.

FRENCH 2—Daniel Mostow, Benjamin L. Gelerman, Leonard Wolsky, Lenin A. Baler, Sumner M. Rothstein, Robert A. Driscoll.

FRENCH 3—James A. Ramsey, Leon N. Hurvitz, Isaac G. Kantrovitz, Philip Feldman, Robert E. Zaugg.

HISTORY D—Earle B. Kaufman, Joel Cohen, Robert J. P. Donlan, Sanford J. Freedman, Philip Feldman, Jacob C. Levenson.

MATHEMATICS BETA—Daniel G. Mostow, Daniel Gorenstein, Morton Waldfogel, Lester M. Abelman, Robert A. Driscoll, Robert Kagan, Herman E. Grossman, Frederick G. Plett, Charles Ginsberg, Sumner M. Rothstein, Walter V. Collins, Gerard W. Renner, Robert M. White, Mario D. Banus, Leonard Walsky, Meredith G. Kline, Arthur M. Ross, Merton H. Miller, Arthur J. Muriph, Leonard A. Caplan, Edward E. Walker.

MATHEMATICS GAMMA—Joseph A. Zilber, Martin F. Bloom, Robert A. Isaacs, John F. Fennessey, Gilbert P. Manet, Samuel N. Harris.

MATHEMATICS A—James J. Fadden.

PHYSICS—Joseph A. Zilber, Sanford J. Friedman, Jacob C. Levenson, Earle B. Kaufman.

CHEMISTRY—John F. Fennessey.

GREEK—Leon Hurvitz.

University of Vermont

Abraham Swartz, a sophomore at the University of Vermont, recently received an award for being wrestling champion of the 145-pound class at Intramural Day.

Bates

Among those recently receiving Bates College intramural athletic awards was David Goldenberg, who graduated from Boston Latin in 1938. Goldenberg qualified for his award by winning the high-jump event in the first annual intramural indoor track meet. At present Goldenberg is hard at work in the baseball cage. "Dave" has put in his bid for a share of the catching assignments and should see quite a bit of service in view of his last year's experience. Harry Gorman, now a member of the junior class at Bates has, this winter been one of the most valuable cogs in Coach "Buck" Spink's varsity basketball team. Gorman was one of the best shots on the team.

*   *

From the "Blue and Gold"—
Blessings on thee, modern maid,
Packed with "oomph" and unafraid.
With your shiny, sheer, silk hose,
And your "très chic" cut-out toes;
With your blood-red lacquered claws
And chapeaux by Lizzie Hawes;
With your sweeping fake eye-lashes,
And your sheath gowns minus sashes;
With your oh—so guiltless gaze,
And a poise no one else can phase;
With your bold, flirtatious eyes
That plays havoc with "us guys"!
For girls like you I am a fan,
But thank the Lord, I Am A Man!

Courting Etiquette or How Time Changes Things
1892: Good evening, Mrs. Smith. Is Mary ready?
1940: Honk! Honk.
1892: You're a vision of loveliness to-night.
1940: Hot dawg! Ain't you the cat?
1892: You dance like an angel.
1940: Boy! You're in the truck, lil bug.
1892: Won't you let me see you home in my horse and buggy?
1940: Hop in the ol' crate, babe, and we'll sputter home.
—The North Star.

RAMBLINGS OF THE REGISTER'S RAVING REPORTER

March 26: The members of the Highway Safety Club took home this moral to-day:

"Here lies the body of Wm. Jay
Who died maintaining his right of way;
He was right, dead right, as he sped along,
But he's just as dead, as if he'd been wrong."

March 27: At the Classical Club meeting to-day, members listened to a discussion of Roman profession. It is claimed that the "Six Little Toga-Makers," tailor their ghost clothing on Via Quinque.

March 28: At about 8:45 to-day a group of idlers about the library witnessed an exciting spectacle. One of the supporting ropes of the flag that hangs outside the library had broken, and all sorts of long poles were brought into play before the stars and stripes were finally captured. Then with a cheer, the idlers moved away—to find themselves late for the first period.

March 29: The R.R.R. didn't go, but R.R.S. (Raving Reporter's Stooge) reported that Mr. O'Leary's protegés conducted themselves in true Latin School fashion in their debate with B. C. High.

April 1: To-day being April Fool's Day, The R.R.R., in making out his year-book record, put down, besides belonging, unofficially, to every club in the school, the Booby prize, the Detention prize, the Door Prize, and the prize for being the smartest moron in the school.

April 2: With the usual prohibitives (no eating, no running, no ball playing) the yard was thrown open to "outdoor recess."—Those who could withstand the mighty blasts ventured out. The R.R.R. stayed in to wait for Spring.

April 3: Meeting of Class I: Hollywood, it is reported, is looking for Mr. Dunn's "five stars," who gave such a remarkable "command" performance.

April 4: The six-for-two-bits pictures that were taken of us last month are not enough; now they are giving us pass cards with numbers on them. . . . They call them 'special assignment cards'. If I had the wings of an angel, o'er these high pr . . .

April 5: At the "Mikado": We won't say that the boys were a little nervous, but we did notice that one lanky individual, whose last initial is Jacobson, was shaking so much that his forehead was coming off (or was that a whig?).

April 9: Banner Club to-day: Special meeting of the Aviation Club; Gorenstein spoke at the Math Club; and the History Club had the pleasure to listen to Mr. Potash a graduate of the Class of 1937, speaking on Latin America.

April 10: We heard, practised, and sang our Class Song for the first time, or was it 'Home Sweet Home! . . . Mr. Cheetham was carried away by his enthusiasm in conducting; in fact, he almost threw himself off the platform. Well. we'll be Senior Class Day . . . and hearing you too.

April 11: To-day, Class I passed a

milestone (or Millstone) in their lives. For one simoleon and six-bits some of us attended the Class Banquet at the Hotel Westminster. Now, we know how to get our cars out of a mud rut in the middle of the North Dakotan desert in the middle of a blinding sandstorm—thanks to Mr. Glover.

April 12: After the memorable way in which Prexy Hoar conducted the Class Day exercises, perhaps it is to be expected that Class I 'pass out' to the tune of Auld Lang Syne. Attorney-General Dever addressed us and spoke about the dark European outlook. . . Just a few days after visiting the Latin School, Mr. Dever announced his candidacy for the Governorship of Massachusetts. Could the fact that the R.R.R. hadn't shaved that morning have any influence on his decision?

April 22: And now that momentous occasion, the deadline of the final issue of THE REGISTER . . . so, boys, get ready with those tomatoes as The R.R.R. takes off his dark glasses and peeks out from behind that mask of dry wit and wet humor.

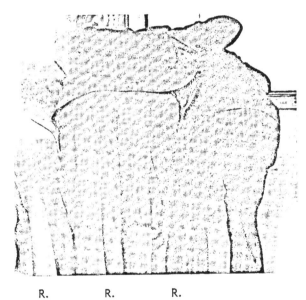

R.   R.   R.

Brown - Prosner - Abelman

Answers to "You're Not So Smart" Quiz

1. Mr. Powers	100	Gaudeamus igitur
2. Highway Safety Club	90	Shark beats you out—sorry
3. Civil War	80	Harvard! Fair Harvard!
4. Henry Lee Higginson	70	Anyway better than 60
5. Stephen Stavro	60	Fair, should do better
6. Mr. Pennypacker	50	Cum Fortuna
7. 850	40	Could Class I do better?
8. Jack Levenson	30	Don't lose hope
9. Mr. Rosenthal	20	There's still a chance
10. Headmaster Gould	10	Not much now
	0	Try again next year

BERTRAM A. HUBERMAN, '40

LET'S CALL IT QUIPS

Words of Wisdom

Look our for your tongue. It's in a wet place and likely to slip.

Heard at the class banquet: "I know where you can get a real chicken dinner for only 25c."

"Where?"

"At the feed store."

A college student returning to the dorm from a date one night found a note from his roommate, which read as follows: "If I'm studying when you get back, wake me up."

He: Do you want to marry a one-eyed man?

She: "No; why?"

He: "Then let me carry your umbrella."

"Have you an opening for a bright, energetic college graduate?"

"Yes, and don't slam it on your way out."

Also at the class banquet: "This waiter is like a fire extinguisher—you have to tip him before you get any service."

"Yes, dad, I'm a big gun up at college."

"Well then, why don't I hear better reports?"

Prof.: "Why don't you answer me?"

Student: "I shook my head."

Prof.: "Well, do you expect me to hear it rattle way up here?"

No matter how far you walk, you move only two feet.

"It's so simple," modestly explains one of the physics assistants, "to hook up power circuits. I merely fasten leads on terminals and pull the switch. If the motor runs, we take our readings. If it smokes, we sneak it back and get another."

One fellow who is sure that men came from monkeys is the man who sweeps up the peanut shells after the ball game.

"Son, every time you get into trouble, I get another grey hair."

"You musta been awful. Look at grandpa."

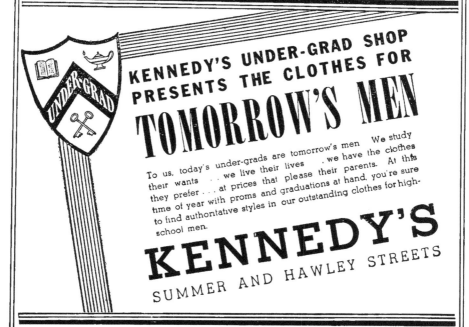

Scholastic Jewelers

INC.

"Official Jewelers of Class of 1940"

5174-78 Washington Street   Boston

Please mention THE REGISTER

Warren Kay Vantine
Studios

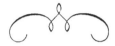

OFFICIAL PHOTOGRAPHER FOR
CLASS OF 1940

160 Boylston Street

Boston, Mass.

The business staff of the Boston Latin School Register wish to express their appreciation to all those advertisers who by their assistance and support have made this magazine possible, and in turn earnestly requests the students of Public Latin School, especially the Class of 1940, to continue to patronize these concerns.

CPSIA information can be obtained
at www.ICGtesting.com
Printed in the USA
BVHW041121211218

536175BV00005B/30/P